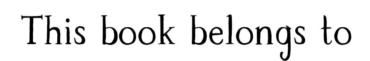

This book belongs to

....

First published 2022 by Macmillan Children's Books
an imprint of Pan Macmillan
The Smithson, 6 Briset Street, London EC1M 5NR
EU representative: Macmillan Publishers Ireland Limited,
1st Floor, The Liffey Trust Centre, 117–126 Sheriff Street Upper, Dublin 1, D01 YC43
Associated companies throughout the world

www.panmacmillan.com

ISBN: 978-1-5290-9292-9

A CIP catalogue record for this book is available
from the British Library.

Printed in China

This Little MONSTER

Coral Byers   Alberta Torres

Macmillan Children's Books

This little monster
goes outside

1

This little monster comes too

2

This little monster
runs ahead...

3

And this little monster shouts

BOO!

4

This little monster tries a treat...

5

This little monster
plays a trick!

6

This little monster
counts the pumpkins…

How many pumpkins
will they pick?

7

This little monster
goes exploring...

8

This little monster's
feeling brave!

This little monster spies
something scary…

What is hiding in the cave?

10

And all the little monsters go...

Reading Together
Tips for Parents and Carers

This book has been specially created and developed for preschool children. It uses the popular nursery rhyme *This Little Piggy* to create an instantly familiar, read-aloud preschool adventure!

- The fun, repetitive and rhythmic text helps develop language and vocabulary.

- The bar along the bottom counts from 1 to 10, with numbers on each page to help children recognise numerals.

- There is a page at the back of the book with more information about the children, to give extra talking points about different personalities, likes and dislikes, and opinions.

- There is plenty of evidence to show that sharing books and reading together helps children to communicate, develop ideas and understanding, and gives them a head start at school. But the most important thing is to enjoy the closeness of sharing a book together.

SCREEEEEEEEEE

EEEAM!

All the way home!

When you read this book together, you could talk to your child about...

... the ten children in the book. Can your child find and count each one as you go along? **What is each child doing?** You could encourage your child to join in and mimic the children's actions.

... how the children's world changes into **an imaginative make-believe world** as they play. What can your child see change as they turn the pages?

... things around you that your child could use to **create their own make-believe world.** What would they like to dress up as?

... the numbers in the book – can they find and **read each number?** Try reading the book while your child counts each little monster on their fingers or toes, just like in the nursery rhyme.

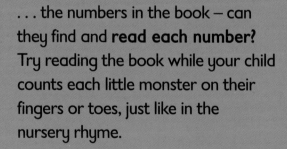

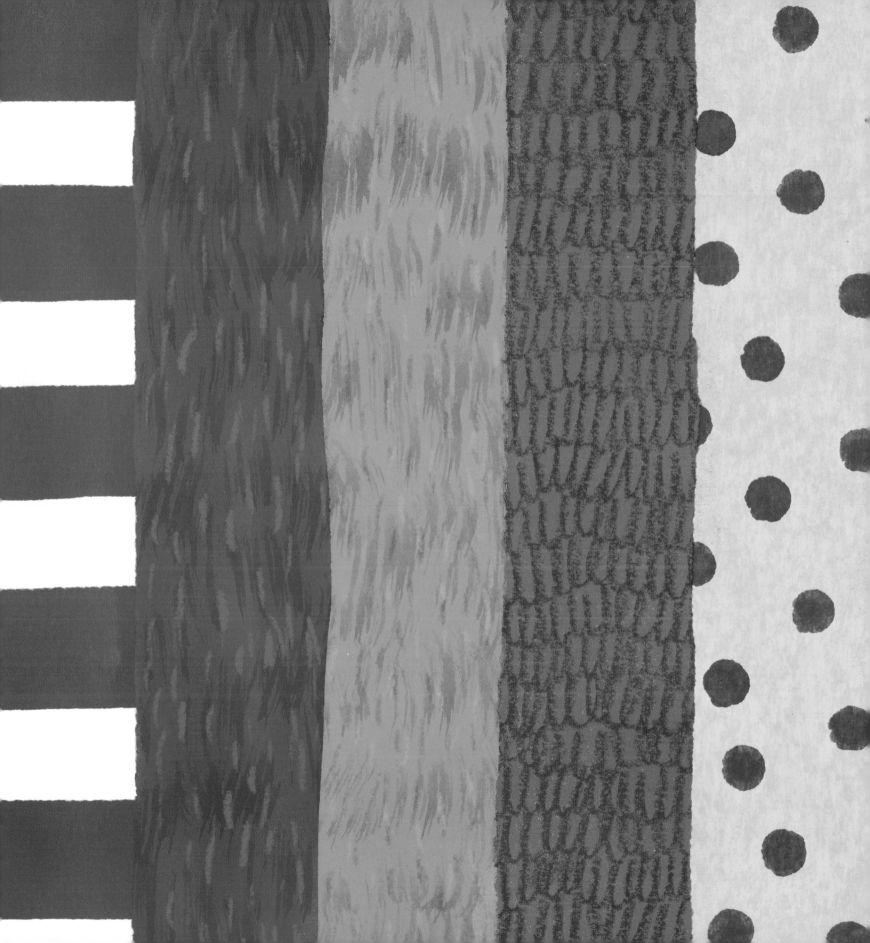

Say Hello to the Monsters!

1 **Noa** loves baking cakes with her daddy.

2 **Muhammed** can get dressed all by himself!

3 **Iris** likes eating broccoli but doesn't like peas.

4 **Max** has a baby sister called Annie.

5 **Evie's** favourite animal is a cat.

6 **Ezra** can pull very funny faces.

7 **Aisha** likes to go really high on the swings.

8 **Grace** is learning to read books all by herself!

9 **Felix's** favourite colour is green.

10 **Benjamin** loves fire engines!

What will they all dress up as next?